Young Welsh Proud

Edited by
Llŷr Titus
and
Megan Angharad Hunter

Published by Dragon Press Ltd, an imprint of Rily Publications Ltd, PO Box 257, Caerphilly CF83 9FL

www.rily.co.uk

Copyright © Dragon Press Ltd 2024

Illustrations © Mari Phillips 2024
Cover artwork and front cover design © Mari Phillips 2024
Back cover and book design: Richard Pritchard

The right of the contributors and Mari Phillips to be identified as the authors and illustrator of this work has been asserted by them in accordance with the Copyright, Designs and Patents Act, 1988 (United Kingdom).

All rights reserved

The publisher acknowledges the funded support of the Books Council of Wales and the Welsh Government.

ISBN: 978-1-80416-405-1

No part of this publication may be reproduced, stored in a retrieval system, or transmitted, in any form, or by any means, electrical, mechanical, photocopying, recording or otherwise without the prior written permission of the publisher or a licence permitting restricted copying. In the United Kingdom such licences are issued by the Copyright Licensing Agency, Saffron House, 6–10 Kirby Street, London EC1N 8TS.

A catalogue record of this book is available from the British Library.

Printed and bound by Ashfords.

CONTENTS

Introduction	7
Brennig	8
Lois	12
Aeron	16
Llŷr	20
Rhiannon	24
Nia	28
Megan	32
Martha	36
Anest	42
Mei	46
Leo	50
Iseult	54
Loti	58
A Timeline of Welsh Queer History	62
What is Pride?	87
How this book came about	88
Support	92
LGBTQIA+ Organisations	93

INTRODUCTION

Every queer person has their story. Sometimes, sadly, because the world is how it is, not every story is a happy one, or some might have more difficult parts than others. But, whatever someone's story is, it deserves to be shared.

That was our idea when we started out with this book; sharing our stories as a community. There are many reasons for that: to help people who might not know much about us to learn; to offer hope to those who are beginning their journey; or to celebrate all sorts of experiences and to be honest about what it's like to be queer in Wales today.

Llŷr's main reason for co-editing and contributing was that he wanted to create the type of book he would have liked to read when he was young. The type of book that could have helped him.

Megan's reason was that she wanted young people to feel less lonely, less isolated, on their journey. The teenage years are difficult enough and the urge to fit in with your peers can sometimes be overwhelming. So Megan hopes that this book will be a comfort to young people and a safe space for them to start to discover who they are, to learn more about their community and to realise that there's a place for them in Wales – a place where they truly belong.

Both of us have been so, so fortunate with the contributors – not only for their company, but because they trusted us with their personal stories. We've enjoyed reading the contributions so much and we're very excited to share them with you now!

So we hope you'll enjoy, learn or sympathise as you read, and hopefully the stories in this book will become a small part of your story as you go on your own journey.

Hwyl,

Llŷr and Megan

My name is Brennig

ABOUT ME

Pronouns: He/Him

From: Vale of Glamorgan

Interests: Reading, writing, running, listening to music, walking the dog

Sexuality: I probably like the word "queer" best

Three words to describe yourself: Likes laughing lots

MY FAVOURITE THINGS

Favourite song: Either 'Hounds of Love' by Kate Bush or 'Atlantic City' by Bruce Springsteen (hard to choose!)

Favourite animal: Dogs.

What do you do? I took a career break to do some travelling (which is a nice way of saying "unemployed"), but before that I worked in a castle (!).

WHY ARE YOU CONTRIBUTING TO THE ANTHOLOGY?

There needs to be more LGBTQ+ representation in Wales, and I'm really pleased and proud to get to contribute to that in any way possible.

Hiraeth[1]

I have always felt *hiraeth*, been homesick. I thought that the first time I felt it was when I moved to Oxford in 2018, to study English. All around me were sharp corners and tight alleyways, when I wanted wide expanses; I wanted the bracken and wild wind of the mountain on which my grandparents live; the sweep of Whitmore Bay, the roar of its sea; the Prince of Wales on a match day, the throng and thrum of accents I recognised, telling jokes I'd heard before that still made me laugh.

But this *hiraeth* made me realise that I'd been homesick long before this, too. That desperate tug and yearning was the same when I was seven, on the schoolyard with a friend. She said that her older brother didn't want her hanging out with me and "my kind of people". I didn't know, then, who "my people" were, what "kind" I belonged to, only that it was wrong, shameful, that one day it might leave me friendless. I noticed myself feeling ways I shouldn't, about people I shouldn't, and as we got older I watched my friends fall in and out of love, kissing, talking freely about whom they might fancy, and I watched it all like I was standing outside, looking in through a window to a house where everyone was cosy and laughing and normal.

There were times when I thought the *hiraeth* – both kinds – might kill me, but it didn't. Being away from Wales forced me out of my shell, to face who I was in the mirror. And I realised that the two things I was – Welsh and queer – could coexist, because the *hiraeth* was native to both experiences, that they were both, as Gwyn Thomas says of home in "*Yma Y Mae Fy Lle*", "*hyd lefelau dyfnaf fy mod*" ("along the deepest levels of my being").

When you think about it, queerness and Welshness are not that far apart: both relatively small, sidelined communities, embattled and defiant, defined and choosing to define ourselves as Other (I am not straight, and I am not English). I'm only half-joking when I say that Dafydd Iwan's "*Yma O Hyd*" isn't a million miles away at all – in its lyrics, sentiment, and even its tune – from Gloria Gaynor's "I Will Survive". And I'll always think of Professor Laura McAllister refusing to remove her rainbow bucket hat in Qatar: that proud, brave, beautiful insistence on the right to be either identity, but most importantly to be both.

I've learnt, over the years, that it's a privilege to be homesick. You only feel *hiraeth* when you love what you have and your home is your home, and you feel there's nothing like it. I was born here, and born the way I was, and I can't pull either strand out of me; they're woven together and threaded like a traditional – sequinned – shawl that I'm delighted to wear over my shoulders.

I have always been homesick, but it's a *hiraeth* that comes from being both Welsh and queer, and so I hold on to it. I know that, in that *hiraeth*, there's a home that one day I'll be able to go back to: I'll walk up the long drive and knock, and the people already inside might say, "What's taken you so long? We've missed you." And I'll know that I've missed them too, so badly, but there'll be lights and music and cake, and this is a house – more than any other house – into which I know I'll always be invited.

[1] *Hiraeth* = yearning, nostalgia, wistfulness, homesickness, earnest desire

My name is Lois

ABOUT ME

Pronouns: She/Her

From: Cwm Croes near Llanuwchllyn, but have been living in Cardiff for over a decade.

Interests: Music (mainly guitar), composing, being outdoors/in nature, writing.

Sexuality: Lesbian

Three words to describe yourself: Thoughtful, creative, mischievous.

MY FAVOURITE THINGS

Favourite song: Oooh. Changes every day. But I'm always a fan of 'Dirty Work' by Steely Dan; 'Helplessly Hoping' by Crosby, Stills and Nash; or 'Our House' by Crosby, Stills, Nash & Young.

Favourite animal: Turtle.

What do you do? Researcher for Public Health Wales and some lecturing/songwriting and performing.

WHY ARE YOU CONTRIBUTING TO THE ANTHOLOGY?

Visibility is so, so important - seeing a book like this, especially by Welsh people, would've really helped me understand who I was when I was younger. It's wonderful to see so much visibility in the media these days, but I still think it's important for everyone to learn about the real experiences of real people from similar backgrounds to themselves as they embark on the journey of getting to know and accept themselves. Getting to contribute towards that in a small way means a lot.

Take your time

The clock and I have never been good friends. I'm always running late, and I've always felt like time was galloping on at a pace I could never quite match. The clock's hands don't reserve their poking and prodding just for when I'm trying to leave the house on time either. They often point out how my path through life is all zigzagged compared to my friends'. Everyone else's timelines seem to flow so neatly and tidily, as straight and steady as a Roman road, while mine is more like Spaghetti Junction.

It's very easy to believe that you're always a little bit behind when you're queer. The clock doesn't stop while you stumble your way through the labyrinth of self-discovery. By the time you reach the end (if there is such a thing), it feels like everyone else has long since forged ahead on their own life paths, while you're miles behind, and you have to hurry to try and catch up.

Feeling that way isn't unique to LGBTQ+ people, of course. It's a common struggle – the ever-persisting process of comparison with everyone else and where they're at with Life's Great Milestones. Graduation. Buying a house. Marriage. Having children. But there's definitely some element of being LGBTQ+ that can make our journeys towards these milestones more convoluted, or leads us to diverge from them entirely.

We all discover things about ourselves throughout our lives, and we often have to work hard to find the answers and accept them. It took a lot of effort for me to come to terms with my sexuality, and it took time. I came out quietly (and drunkenly) to my best friend, about a month after coming out of a five-year straight relationship. I'd started noticing the signs long before that, but acknowledging them almost felt like cheating. I was afraid of losing everything, so I buried the feelings deep inside until the relationship ended. I was twenty-four then, and I was twenty-five when my first queer relationship began.

It was very easy to feel that I'd lost precious time along the way. All those years I could have spent being the real me. All the years ahead of me where I'd need to rebuild my life from scratch. These thoughts still linger in my head sometimes. But when I catch myself feeling this way, the idea of "queer time" is one that offers me a lot of comfort.

The idea conveys how the queer experience transforms our relationship with time. Traditional society has an expectation of what Life's Great Milestones are. There's also an expectation that they happen in a linear way, and that we mature slowly through them all. Birth, childhood, teens, growing into adulthood, finding a partner, raising children. Not everyone follows the formula, of course. But how might being queer affect this linear trajectory?

Coming out felt like a kind of rebirth for me. And even though I'd been in quite a serious relationship with a guy the year before, I was like a teenager in my first relationship with a girl because everything was so new and exciting. I was rediscovering myself. Rematuring. Playfully breaking down the straight and narrow path that had led me astray for as long as I could remember.

That process ate into my twenties, of course. My friends were getting engaged, marrying and having extremely cute babies. And compared to them and considering where I had been a couple of years earlier, I sometimes felt like I had just landed on a snake on the last square in a game of Snakes and Ladders. But, in reality, I'd just climbed the wrong ladder on the first roll of the dice.

We all carve our own unique paths through life. Like adventurers discovering new lands, only we can set the time goals for journeys no one else has trodden before. I find it so easy to look back and resent the fact that I've been so slow, or wasted my time. It's harder to be kind to yourself and accept that time is the best tool for carving out the path ahead of us. But that's the only way forward. So wherever you are on your own journey, take your time and celebrate all the precious little moments that have led you along the way.

My name is Aeron

ABOUT ME

Pronouns: They/Them/He/Him

From: Llandysul

Interests: Researching politics, listening to music and spending time with friends

Sexuality: Bisexual

Three words to describe yourself: Confident, funny and kind

MY FAVOURITE THINGS

Favourite song: 'From the Start' or 'Atlas' by Good Kid

Favourite animal: Dogs.

What do you do? Studying Criminology, Psychology and Welsh for A level and I also volunteer with Plethu, a community-driven creative well-being project.

WHY ARE YOU CONTRIBUTING TO THE ANTHOLOGY?

Sharing our stories is one of the best ways to connect and bring an understanding to topics that are often overlooked. By sharing, I hope to make a difference to those who may be insecure or curious, and help spark real conversations.

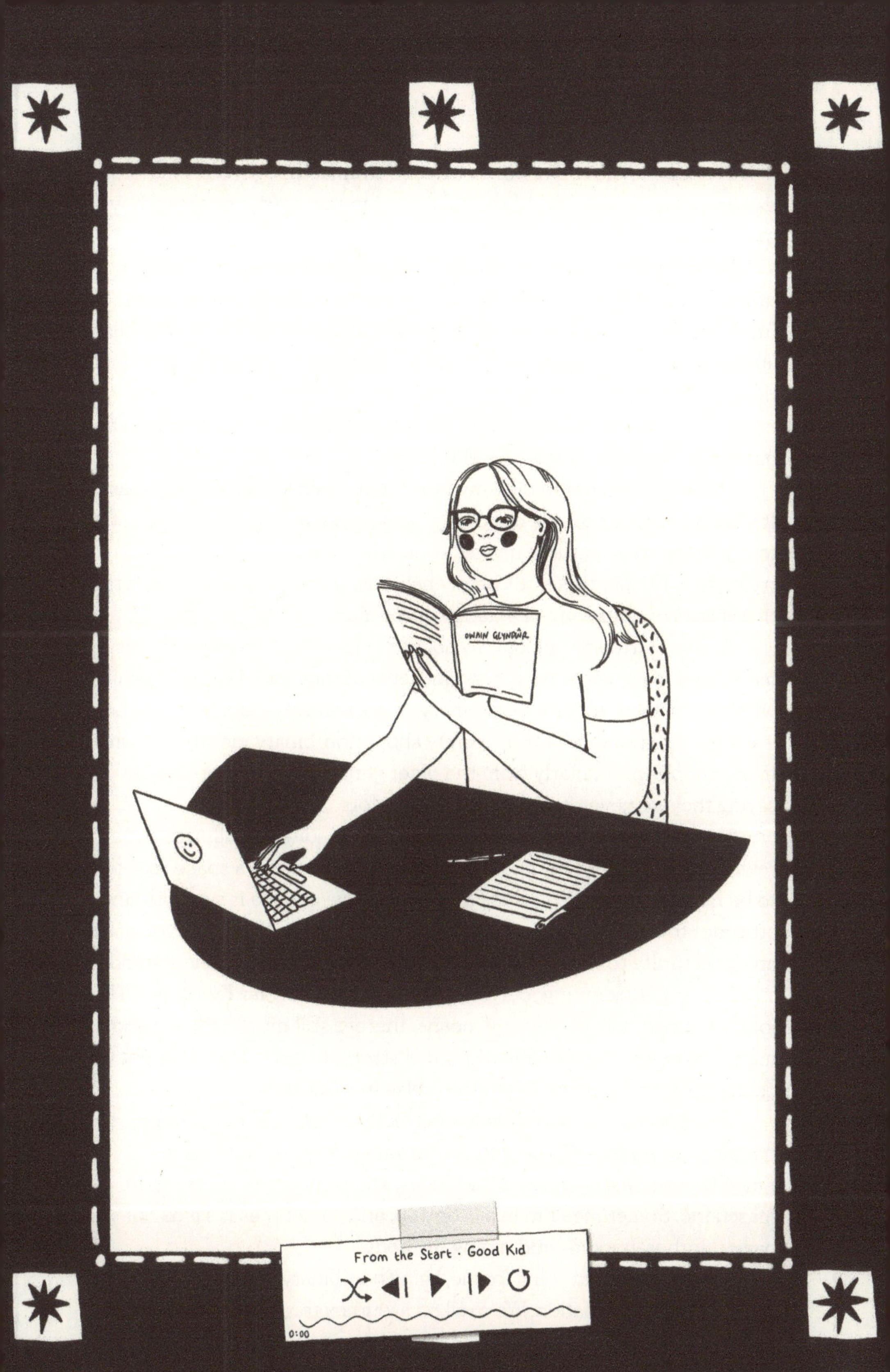
OWAIN GLYNDŴR
From the Start · Good Kid
0:00

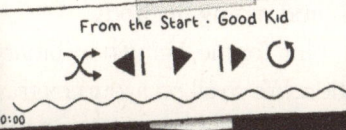

I'm Aeron, and I'm non-binary. And that's who I am, in a simple little sentence.

The journey to today hasn't been so simple, though, but I'm here, existing exactly how I feel I should exist. I'm not a girl, nor am I a boy. I'm me – without barriers.

For many years, I've questioned my gender. Even when I was in primary school, I was uncomfortable in my body. It's been a journey from feeling utterly terrible while battling all these emotions, to feeling absolute relief in sharing who I truly am with my friends. I'm lucky that they, and my family, are incredibly supportive. There are, of course, a few exceptions, such as name-calling from other people every now and then, but that's thankfully a very small minority.

Exploring and embracing my non-binary identity hasn't been easy. It's been a journey of self-discovery, on which I've had to learn to listen to the inner-most parts of myself, even when the noise of the world is trying to suffocate them. It's been challenging and beautiful, in a world that insists on imposing neat labels on us all.

As I've started to talk openly about my identity, I've realised that many people are eager to understand, even if they aren't initially familiar with the concept of being non-binary. It has recently emerged that there is complete ignorance within society about non-binary identities – with many people, particularly from the older generations, responding by saying they've never heard of the term before.

The process of educating others has been quite a challenge but a rewarding one. If I'm honest about who I am, it creates a space for others to be honest about themselves as well. Positive change is possible, and attitudes towards gender are evolving, albeit slowly. Every conversation is an opportunity to challenge prejudices and gain a deeper understanding.

Looking back on my journey so far, I realise how far I've come. The journey is not over yet, by any means; there is still much to learn and many obstacles to overcome. But I feel stronger and more confident with each step. I could never be anything else in this world.

It's important to note that it's perfectly normal for non-binary people's experiences to be different from each other. Sometimes I'm glitzy and wear rings and necklaces, and sometimes I dress more masculine. Sometimes I'm in a crop-top, and sometimes it's a day of baggy clothes, hoodies and hiding my body.

But the important thing for me, being non-binary, is that I can be myself – without any explanation. We're all on a journey through life, and we all have to fight through every challenge, embrace the fun, and do our best to be at our best when we can. No matter who or what we are.

How can you be supportive? Here are some simple steps:

- Everyone has two ears to listen – if someone reveals to you that they are gay, non-binary or trans, or whatever, be kind and be supportive. And ask what their preferred pronouns are and use them. There will be mistakes along the way at first, of course, but being supportive and considerate is so, so important. This includes any name change, too. I have a new name that is different from the name on my birth certificate – and that's the name I want everyone to call me from now on.
- Use the correct vocabulary. There is a useful list on the Stonewall Cymru website.
- Creating a safe and welcoming atmosphere is also vital, and not being judgemental. It's OK to ask questions – and ask more if there's a misunderstanding. Don't discount feelings – and remember: the experiences of everyone in the LGBTQ+ community aren't the same.
- You must be true to the individual's desires, too. If someone turns to you and trusts you and doesn't want anyone else to know, you have to respect that. Unless, of course, they feel very depressed and want to harm themselves. At that point, you must turn to a teacher, family member or professional person so they can get the right support.
- Challenge. Challenging homophobia, biphobia and transphobia is a priority. If you come across this behaviour, you have to say something and not sweep the ugly comments under the carpet. Always be supportive, speak up and educate others when they are cruel.
- No one is perfect, but we can all help each other so that LGBTQ+ people can live in a world that accepts and embraces us.

It's important for individuals like me, and all of us, to continue to fight for equality and acceptance in our communities. By sharing our stories and speaking openly, we can help build a more inclusive and loving world for everyone, regardless of identity.

It would be nice to live in a world where gender diversity is celebrated, not just tolerated. A future in which non-binary individuals can thrive, without fear of discrimination or harm.

I want to be free to express my true self openly and joyfully.

> My name is **Llŷr**

ABOUT ME

Pronouns: He/Him

From: Pen Llŷn

Interests: Walking, cooking, binding books, reading (mainly sci-fi, horror and fantasy), watching films, beekeeping, gardening.

Sexuality: Bisexual.

Three words to describe yourself: Loyal, stubborn, messy.

MY FAVOURITE THINGS

Favourite song: 'Glaw' by Cowbois Rhos Botwnnog.

Favourite animal: Cat.

What do you do? Writer, editor, director.

WHY ARE YOU CONTRIBUTING TO THE ANTHOLOGY?

Because I want to create a book that I would've liked to read when I was younger.

It's quite a common thing to ask what you'd say to a younger version of yourself; in fact, it was one of the things we discussed when we were thinking about this book. And when I think about the young Llŷr Titus as I remember him – that teenager who, even though he had good friends, was bullied and saw himself as someone on the sidelines more often than not – I can't think of an answer. He'd be surprised, I'm sure, that he's a part of a book like this one.

It took me a while to sort myself out and get a full and confident grasp of my sexuality. Where I'm from and my background has a part in that, I think. Of course I feel very grateful to my community back home and my family, because they were all, on the whole, supportive. But, at school and in the wider community, there was a lack of diversity and understanding, and a culture that was drenched in toxic masculinity.

It's not surprising then that it took me a while to get to know myself – there was work to do unwrapping, discovering and learning.

Though I knew – or supposed – I was bi, I didn't *know* either, if that makes sense. I was a very keen "ally" and happily so for a while. Everyone can appreciate the beauty of people no matter their sex or gender, can't they? That's what I thought, anyway. Everyone fancies a wide range of people and boys get crushes on other boys sometimes, right? These were the little stories I told myself. It's easy thinking back to see all these things and realise how I wasn't being honest with myself – for example, even though I was a big fan of sci-fi there was another reason I was such a fan of David Tennant in *Doctor Who*, wasn't there? But I never got a bright, light-bulb flash – it was a lot more like an energy-saving bulb slowly warming up.

Talking of sci-fi, I'm quite fond of the many-worlds interpretation, or the idea of multiverses – that there are many universes that exist beyond our own. So, in this theory, there's an infinite number of universes and an infinite number of *me*s, with each version being different.

There's a universe where I came out much earlier; one where I understood myself earlier; another one where the early years of my teenage life in a rural area were so much easier; another where there wasn't any bullying – where I got to keep my self-confidence and grow it. There's one within spitting distance, where I feel like I've fitted in my own skin since day one. There must be, right?

But there are ones where I'm not out at all, ones where I never understand myself or my sexuality – there are ones where I deny who I am.

I'm in this universe, the one where you're reading this book, right now, and that's perfectly fine. It's good. I am where I am and I've experienced everything I have and that's why I am who I am, here, now. It's possible that there's a perfect Llŷr out there, and good on him, I say. I am who I am and that's OK as well. A jumper doesn't complain because it's got a few stitches missing or a crooked arm; it's knitted the way it's knitted.

Something else I think about is how maybe every version of me could meet in a dream or in a world between worlds. In a huge amphitheatre, maybe, or in a field so big that you can only see the hedges if you gaze towards the horizon. A field full of buttercups and tall grass with a slight breeze and a bright sky. And we'll all be there, every Llŷr – from the most perfect to the least, with me somewhere in the middle. We'll each have our place there and each of us will deserve it – no matter the mistakes or the successes we've had. Because all of us are valid and have a right to be who we are – no matter what anyone else says.

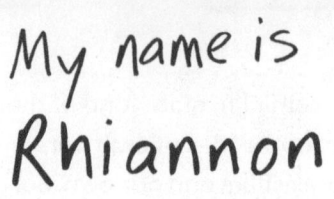

My name is Rhiannon

ABOUT ME

Pronouns: She/Her

From: South Wales

Interests: Video-gaming and cooking

Sexuality: Queer

Three words to describe yourself: Caring, funny, bubbly

MY FAVOURITE THINGS

Favourite song: 'Anything But Me' by MUNA

Favourite animal: Cat!

What do you do? Studying Psychology and Criminology

WHY ARE YOU CONTRIBUTING TO THE ANTHOLOGY?

I wanted to contribute to the book because it sounded like a fun opportunity to do something I'd never done before, and the concept of the book was something I'd never seen out there before and would love to be a part of.

My name is Rhiannon, I'm twenty-one years old and I've lived my whole life in a small, conservative village in South Wales. Coming out was not easy, but I'd like to focus on the positive experiences I've had, because I don't feel like they're talked about enough. When I was coming to terms with who I was, I was bombarded with stories of people being disowned because of who they were, and it scared me. Of course, this does happen sometimes and it's horrible, but I've had some really great experiences because and in spite of the fact that I'm gay, experiences I didn't always believe I deserved. There are pros and cons to everything in life, but if I can help one young person feel a little brighter about their future, I'll be happy.

When I was thirteen, I had my first "gay love". I'd had boyfriends before, but I always felt indifference towards them, rather than anything close to resembling love. This new experience made me realise I was gay. Understanding who I was felt like how I imagine a flower feels in spring, when it blooms and feels the sun on its petals for the first time. I felt like I was finally awake. It sounds like a cliché but, in that moment, everything was so pure and I wasn't scared because I felt so right.

When I moved to university, my gay identity was very important to me. I spent my first university year in Huddersfield, a town in the north of England. I made my first "gay friends" in Huddersfield. We would hang out and chat about gay things, things I wouldn't have shared with non-LGBT people because I felt they wouldn't have understood. It's a very freeing feeling when you find people that can relate to you. We went to gay bars together and danced with drag queens. We experienced things I never thought I'd be able to experience, just because of who I was.

But I'm a home-body and a Welsh girl through and through, so I transferred from Huddersfield to Swansea University. I experienced Swansea in a very different way than I did Huddersfield. I felt as though I'd done a lot of self-discovery and reflection during my first year of university, so when I came to Swansea my LGBT identity didn't feel like such a big deal. I felt more comfortable in myself thanks to the friends I'd made in Huddersfield; I felt validated by them. I also felt secure because I was now closer to my support network at home. I never knew how much I could miss Welsh road signs!

I met my first proper girlfriend when I was eighteen. Bringing her into my life was daunting – I'd never even introduced my parents to a boyfriend so I was worried about how they'd react, but I'm pleased to say that they treat her in exactly the same way as they treat my brother's wife. It's easy – like, easier than I had ever dreamt it could be.

In my years of coming to accept who I am I've found that I had a lot of internal homophobia to work through. I'd worry that people thought I was disgusting and perverted because those were my own stigmas and opinions that I was projecting on to others. As I have grown up and accepted myself, the fear of other people's judgement has subsided because, as it turns out, the majority of the hatred I was scared of experiencing was coming from inside myself.

I used to feel as though the LGBT aspect of my identity was the outstanding feature of my character. I think I thought I didn't have much else to offer people, but as I have got older, I now feel like a more well-rounded individual. I am extremely proud of where I come from and who I'm becoming. If there was one piece of advice I could give to younger me, it would be to be patient, with yourself and others. Identity is a beautiful thing; please don't hide who you are. It is cliché, but there is no one out there like you.

My name is Nia

ABOUT ME

Pronouns: She/Her

From: Cardiff

Interests: Reading, writing, cycling, travelling, roller-skating, baking

Sexuality: Lesbian.

Three words to describe yourself: Usually I'm optimistic

MY FAVOURITE THINGS

Favourite song: 'Smoke and Ashes' by Tracy Chapman

Favourite animal: Bat!

What do you do? Poet, author, dramaturg and translator

WHY ARE YOU CONTRIBUTING TO THE ANTHOLOGY?

To be a part of the Welsh queer scene that's growing more and more each year!

I feel quite happy about my identity as a queer Welsh person now, but growing up I don't think I was ever able to weave together the idea of being Welsh and speaking Welsh with the idea of being queer. I always thought I'd have to move somewhere else to work out who I was, and then come back. I think that's quite a common feeling amongst queer young people in Wales.

My Welsh and queer identities weave together because the problems I deal with as a lesbian can be similar to the problems I deal with as a person who is half black, half white, and they again can be similar to the problems that I deal with as someone who speaks Welsh. So I always try to remember that everything is interconnected and there's no one problem that stands on its own. As a mixed-race person, I haven't always felt like I fit in with Welsh speakers, but a lot of people are talking about that feeling of not fitting in in Welsh schools and so on now. But I'm always very aware that my experience isn't as bad as it is for people who, for example, wear a hijab or people who have dark skin, because the things they might go through can be a lot worse than what I go through, so I always try to acknowledge that.

I think there's a big part of identity for me that's about family and about routes of ancestry; that's what's important to me. Being someone from Wales, but also someone whose grandmother and grandfather moved from another country to the docks in Cardiff – that's a big part of my identity as well. I've always felt proud to be someone from Wales, but I do think quite a lot about Welsh history and how it's important not to be blindly positive about that history either.

I'm a poet, writer and playwright, and when I'm writing, the characters that come into my head are usually very similar to me, especially when I'm writing for young people. I think a part of me is still trying to process things – the parts of my identity and how they weave together – which is why the themes of my work usually deal with being queer or being mixed-race or feeling like you're not Welsh enough, because that's what I was dealing with when I was at school. Those experiences still flash up now so I try to work through them while writing. And if I've written a play and a young person is watching it and thinking, "That's the exact same thing I'm going through right now," maybe it'll help them, so that's what I'm trying to do. Writing is almost like therapy for me, because I notice things about myself I thought I'd finished with years ago.

When I run workshops with young people, I want to know what makes them feel proud, and what makes them feel like they have roots. Because I'm a person who has a lot of anxiety, one thing that always grounds me is remembering that I'm not the only person in the world who deals with the things that I deal with. It makes me feel like I'm not alone in the world if I remember someone else has gone through this, so then I feel like everything is OK and is going to work out. Knowing that there's a queer community out there helps too because there are anxieties that are more specific to us, and I'm always thinking about how I can retain that feeling of community because I feel like I'm always trying to resist individualism. So because I have a community, if I need help, I can ask for help. I'm fortunate now that I have a circle and a community of friends, most of whom are queer too, so it's nice to know that I have some sort of back-up.

It's important to remember that you're not alone; people go through the same things that you're going through. And I also always try to remember that people, as a whole, are kind. Although the world might feel big and scary sometimes, it's important to remember that people do want to help; I think that's how people are at their core.

My name is Megan

ABOUT ME

Pronouns: She/Her

From: Penygroes, Dyffryn Nantlle, but currently living in Cardiff

Interests: Films, books, baking, writing, music (I play flute, saxophone, guitar and piano)

Sexuality: Bisexual and demisexual

Three words to describe yourself: Creative, sensitive and empathetic

MY FAVOURITE THINGS

Favourite song: Ahhh, it's so hard to choose just one ... or even ten! But these days, I turn quite often to these songs: 'if i were a fish' by corook, 'That Funny Feeling' by Phoebe Bridgers / Bo Burnham, 'Fel i Fod' by Adwaith, 'Life on Earth' by Snow Patrol and 'Bridoll' by Cerys Hafana.

Favourite animal: Cats and dogs

What do you do? Author, screenwriter and children's book editor

WHY ARE YOU CONTRIBUTING TO THE ANTHOLOGY?

I want to increase the visibility of bisexual and ace-spec people.

everyone else living their lives contentedly, belonging as if belonging was easy. But after I discovered demisexuality and the asexual spectrum on the internet, some of those walls were knocked down. I finally began to realise that I wasn't completely "broken" after all.

The acephobia sometimes makes me feel like I don't belong in any circle or community, even queer ones, as the letter "A" is often invisible in the LGBTQ+ acronym. I've turned to hate myself and my "lack" so much that I sometimes worry I'll never be able to rid myself of the self-hatred entirely. But while there's still a lot of misunderstanding about the asexual spectrum, I've recently started to feel something, a shift in the deepest pockets of my heart, and that's due to a growing representation of people on the asexual spectrum, thanks to shows like *Heartstopper* and *Sex Education*. I'm still not entirely proud of my identity, but I've started to come out and have subsequently been introduced to a new community and a sense of acceptance and belonging that I've never felt before.

In 2020 I published a Welsh novel for young people called *tu ôl i'r awyr*. The two main characters in the novel are members of the LGBTQ+ community; one is bi and the other is asexual. At the time, I hadn't come to terms with my relationship with the asexual spectrum – to be honest, I didn't realise the character was asexual until after the book was published – so there isn't a direct mention of the character's asexuality in the novel. But since then, I've had the opportunity to translate my book into English and, in that version, the discussion on asexuality is more prominent. That's proof, I think, that accepting yourself as the real you is possible, with time, however deep your internal phobia has permeated. So I hope that when the English version is eventually published, it will be a comfort to some young people who feel like they don't belong either.

I currently identify as bisexual and demisexual. But to be honest, I've never been too fond of labels because I believe that identity is something fluid that can change and develop over time as you grow and learn more about yourself and the LGBTQ+ community. It's OK if there isn't a flag that represents you and it's OK if you are the plus in the LGBTQ+ acronym. That's what's so wonderful about this community; you don't need a label to belong – you just need to be yourself, wholly, whatever that might be. You *do* belong, whatever you feel or don't feel, and don't let anything take that away from you.

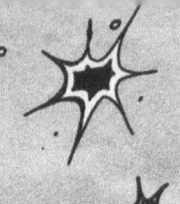

My name is Martha

ABOUT ME

Pronouns: They//Them/She/Her

From: I live in Waunfawr near Caernarfon.

Interests: I'm interested in music, reading, politics and history

Sexuality: Queer

Three words to describe yourself: Funny/strange, hopeful, curious

MY FAVOURITE THINGS

Favourite song: That's a hard question for a DJ! I enjoy many different songs, but at the moment I'm enjoying listening to 'Allwedd' or 'Pen y Mynydd' by Bwncath and 'Graceland Too' by Phoebe Bridgers!

Favourite animal: Pine martens and Hebridean sheep

What do you do? My background's in poetry and the arts – I'm trying to find a way to make them a part of my work.

WHY ARE YOU CONTRIBUTING TO THE ANTHOLOGY?

As a Welsh learner and new writer, this is a great opportunity to make connections with other creative Welsh people and think collectively about Welsh experiences, especially queer ones.

Author's note: I have lived in *Gogledd Cymru* for around three years now, three winters of being surrounded by the ever-changing landscapes of Eryri whilst learning *yr iaith Gymraeg*. Entering into *y gymdeithas Gymraeg* whilst also exploring the personal, internal landscapes of my queerness – in all its non-linear, non-normative ways – has drawn me to write a series of musings on the Trans/*Traws* words and ways of Welsh.

Trawstrefa – Transhumance

The curves of your contours and sheep tracks traverse – hidden paths – shifting maps where we have meandered and talked – escaped to edges – after school together, homework finished, pretences made, then out the back door to meet with you where pine trees and peat meet – the sky comes up to greet us cocooned by mist and moss up the moel with you.

    From Hafod to Hendref and back again – the cycle of the year, the circle of the sun/moon's path ... parts of a whole between here and there.

    This is an acoustic land, the echoes of past eras, people – listen carefully and you may hear their secrets told only to the hills around – with pride from the top of their peaks or with quiet confidence between alcoves and crags ... Fy nghynefin – teimlad of dderbyniad rhwng yr afon a'r môr.

And it's so fleeting and ethereal, points of view in the line of time. Dreaming here, dreaming there. You think you're the first one on the top of a mountain, but there were probably many people there before you.

— Anohni[1]

My hairy calves and your bracken-thicketed flanks   only the mountain and me
   my feet and fingers sink into below ground   freezing under silent moonlight
 scintillating shifting light   our other selves   elsewhere far from others for now
and all the better for it.

    Edrychwch! Glimmers of hope appear ... there's queers in them there (their/they're) hills – the moulding, mossy, mulching, nebulous/niwlog ... chwynnyn mewn agennau – er gwaetha' pawb a phopeth.

[1] Anonhi is a queer performance artist and musician. This quote comes from their article for the *Atmos* online magazine, "On Queer Ecology and Trans Ferality".

Trawsieithu - Trans-languaging

> What name are you known by today?
> Beth yw dy enw heddiw?
> Will I even see you?
> I'w weld.
> When can I see you ...
> Or will you wrap yourself up and brood behind sheets of silken grey moist air ...?
> Dan orchudd o niwl sidanaidd.

Moel Eilio is known by two names – Eilio, supporting the ridge that leads to Yr Wyddfa, and colloquially as the Hill of the Hue ... It changes minute by minute, day by day and season by season. It supports too the track of the moon which rolls up and down the hillside on still, clear nights: Unwaith yn y pedwar amser.

Pan dwi'n torheulo mewn enfys o olau lleuad wrth i mi edrych dros y bryniau liw nos.

Trawsleoliad - Translocation

Pride in Welshness and pride in queerness are not mutually exclusive. Wales is a place where identity is constantly up for debate – ever more so in a time of increasing activism amongst Welsh-language, independence and queer communities – and the intersections between these and other experiences of plural, non-binary (in the broadest sense of the term) Welshness.

Not being a native of Cymru I naturally feel somewhat gwahanol (different) from time to time – an experience not unlike exploring queerness – how do you communicate the complexity of such an experience – y profiad Cymraeg, cwiar neu y naill a'r llall? Yn enwedig pan ydych yn falch o fod yn wledig hefyd.

Trawsnewidiol - Transitional

> The caverns of the old quarries
> will keep our secrets
> For now
> I will tell each piece of slate
> Echoing acknowledgement
> acceptance

Your scars healing, whilst birds wheeling ever overhead – your strength in your staying – you are old and young all at once – wise is the wind – your creation of clouds that roll over and off you.
Resonate, resonant and resolute.

> *Ond fel 'na wyt ti a fel yna ti fod*
> *Does 'na neb arall fel chdi yn bod.* – Bwncath

Trawswladol - Transnational

Cities are not the only answer to finding community in Cymru if you're young and queer – although it might not be the super-social metropolitan experience of people from Caerdydd. The pace of life is slower here … fewer people, more space to breathe, the ability to know one's milltir sgwâr.

> These hills have been here for time
> They've seen it all before
> There is the place:
> Their slope-slate sides
> Known to themselves
> For centuries, millennia
> Before and after
> We all have been through
> The trials, tribulations – tributaries
> Of the valleys below

My name is Anest

ABOUT ME

Pronouns: She/Her

From: Originally from Dyffryn Nantlle, but I'm currently based in Cardiff

Interests: Reading good books, listening to good music, discovering random trivia on Wikipedia (especially of the linguistic kind) and being outdoors.

Sexuality: Bisexual.

Three words to describe yourself: Silly, open-minded, hopeful

MY FAVOURITE THINGS

Favourite song: 'Someone Tell the Boys' by Samia

Favourite animal: My fourteen-year-old black cat Pantera

What do you do? Social researcher

WHY ARE YOU CONTRIBUTING TO THE ANTHOLOGY?

I'm contributing to turn the volume up on bisexual voices here in Wales.

The Bisexual Vantage Point

One evening last winter, my girlfriend, our friend and I were walking towards Cardiff city centre along Newport Road, headed towards an event I can't quite recall. Nor can I recall what we were wearing, but for reference: I've got short, short hair and a pierced septum, and my girlfriend *always* hangs her keys on a carabiner on her hip. With the stereotypical portrayal of a queer woman in mind, it's not hard to deduce that we *might* not be straight. So, three bisexual women were walking down the street. Two girls were headed towards us, and as they approached, one of them pointed down towards our shoes.

"Oh, it looks like you've dropped your—"

We all looked to the ground, prematurely grateful that a stranger would point out whatever it was that one of us had dropped.

"*—gay card.*"

Our gratitude quickly morphed into a shooting sensation of cringe. The unanticipated remark stunned us into silence and in consequence we spent the rest of the walk discussing, with regret, what our ideal, brutal comeback should have been.

I began coming out as bi when I was thirteen years old, and over the years I've found that I'm pretty good at disregarding any biphobia headed my way, whether it's unintentionally concealed within a passing comment, or explicitly hateful. It feels like a peculiar privilege to say that I've received very, very little of the latter kind, and that most of what I've heard first-hand has simply been ignorance, wilful or not. In my experience, it's mostly been covert sexualisation — boys sneaking up to watch as I kissed another girl, girls asking if I'd kiss them so they could impress boys. That sort of thing.

During the last ten years of primarily dating men, I felt somewhat emotionally shielded from those offensive attitudes. The comments never pierced too deeply because they didn't affect my social status, and being in a societally conforming relationship was a safety net in itself. Thanks to the heteronormative nature of our society, I never felt judged for being in a relationship with a man, even if we were both queer. I could hide my queerness behind the relationship if I chose to.

Things changed when I met my girlfriend.

As I fell in love with her, the realisation dawned on me that I would have no choice but to adjust to being wholly visible as a queer woman. The ability to conceal my sexuality behind the straight-passing veneer was no longer there. I noticed that I felt apprehensive about being affectionate with her in public; on one of our first dates, just as we were about to kiss on a vacant lane, I felt a foreboding pinprick of fear as a stranger rounded the corner from Cathays station. We kissed, and nothing happened that time, but unfortunately the incident later on Newport Road validated that apprehension. The kind of apprehension that I never felt with boyfriends.

A great-aunt of mine recently asked if I had a partner: "Is he Welsh?"

"No, but her dad is from Pembrokeshire."

She meant no harm, but it stung nonetheless. As a reminder that heteronormativity still corners people into making assumptions, which in turn corners *us* into staying in the proverbial closet. *If I'm with a man and they think I'm straight, why complicate things?* I'm far from being the only bi person to have felt this. In 2020, Stonewall published its Bi Report, summarising their findings on the experiences of thousands of bisexuals in Britain. In their sample, 80% of bisexual people weren't out to all their family members, and 64% weren't out to their friends — this meant that the bi people were *less than half as likely* to be out as the gay and lesbian people in the study.

The snide girls on Newport Road, the apprehension I felt kissing my girlfriend in public, the act of maintaining a straight-passing narrative ... they all represent the ever-present gulf that separates attitudes towards same-sex and other-sex relationships. To me, bisexuality feels like the vantage point from which I can best observe and experience that gulf.

Although we didn't reach a conclusion regarding which comeback would have burned the best, I'm glad to have firmly reached a point in my life where I'd rather drop my gay card on the floor than be too ashamed to take it out in the first place. I really don't know who I'd be if I wasn't bi.

My name is Mei

ABOUT ME

Pronouns: He/Him/They/Them

From: Pentre'r Bryn, Ceredigion, but now living in London.

Interests: Sewing and designing fancy clothes for festivals!

Sexuality: Queer.

Three words to describe yourself: Sociable. Thoughtful. Nonconforming.

MY FAVOURITE THINGS

Favourite song: It changes constantly but 'Sunset' by Caroline Polachek has been a favourite of mine for a while.

Favourite animal: Giraffe

What do you do? Dance artist: performer, choreographer and movement director.

WHY ARE YOU CONTRIBUTING TO THE ANTHOLOGY?

I believe that documenting creative queer individuals' experiences is an exciting idea. The anthology is full of colourful and lovely people and it's wonderful to get to celebrate that and share our stories.

I came out, got to know myself, came to terms with my sexuality and my identity as a queer person whilst living in London, so this created some sort of discord between two important elements of my identity – my Welshness and my queer identity. I couldn't quite bring the two together at first. Because I came out in London, when I returned to Wales I wasn't quite sure how to exist as a queer person there. But I remember *Mas ar y Maes* (Out on the Field) kicking off at the Cardiff Bay National Eisteddfod in 2018, and the two things clicked and I remember thinking, "Wow, there's a space for queer Welsh people!"

Sometimes identity is unclear, and that's OK. You don't have to know exactly how you identify. I think a vagueness about your identity is probably a good thing. There's this pressure to answer questions like "Who are you?" and "*What are you?*". But if you decide "Well, I'm *this*, but I'm also *this*, and I'm not sure what that is and what it means," that's fine. There's an expectation, this need to stick a label on who you are or what you are, but I think it's also important to note that that can change at any time, or maybe that label contains ten words! It doesn't need to be so black and white; that's the pressure society puts on you. So it's OK to be in the middle, and to change your mind as well.

In my journey of finding out who I am, I've been using the word "queer" to describe myself more and more because it encompasses a lot of different things, and it means I don't have to put a specific label on my sexuality or gender. To me, the word "queer" is all-encompassing and open. The whole of our identity is built out of a lot of different things, I think. There are some things that I'm proud of about myself, like being a Welsh-speaking Welsh person, and a few things that I've grown to be proud of over time, like my identity as a queer person – these are very important elements of my identity. But it's not just those things by themselves – all the elements that make us up weave together into a sort of colourful blanket; all these things are touching each other, connecting and affecting each other, enriching who we are to make this kind of complex (but delicious) lasagne of everything.

    That journey of coming out and discovering myself, tied to being a dancer and someone who uses the body in a variety of creative ways, means that my body now feels like a safe space for me. This is something that, as a queer person, hasn't always been the case. Dancing is a way for me to make some sort of sense of being Welsh and queer. I wasn't really sure how to be in either place – how to be Welsh in London and how to be gay in rural Ceredigion – but dance helped me to work out the connections between the two things. I've created *Qwerin*, a contemporary dance performance that's a celebration of that intertwining. *Qwerin* is a mix of traditional Welsh folk dance and the influences of queer clubbing and nightlife, bringing the two worlds together in a way that interweaves and celebrates cultures and the discovery of community. *Qwerin* places traditional Welsh dance in a new light. But the purpose of the work isn't to undermine the importance of keeping and protecting the tradition in its present form, but rather to challenge traditions and to celebrate the dance in a new form, protecting culture as well as welcoming change.

    There's a place in the world and in Wales for you to be you, and even if you haven't found that place yet, just trust that it exists and that there are people who, in some way, share the same experiences as you. "Queer joy" is a recurring theme in my work and in my daily life; I discover "queer joy" in both places. So I want to tell people that queer joy exists and it can exist for you too; you can find it – it's out there.

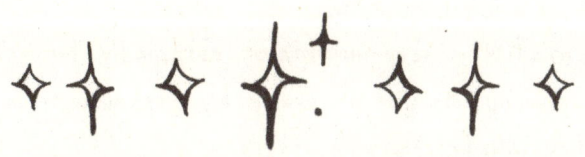

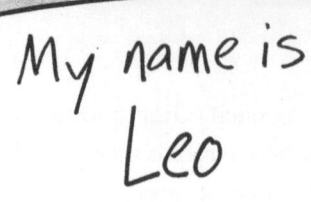

My name is Leo

ABOUT ME

Pronouns: He/Him

From: Cardiff

Interests: Film, theatre, poetry, art

Sexuality: Queer.

Three words to describe yourself: Creative, friendly, fun

MY FAVOURITE THINGS

Favourite song: 'Dos yn dy Flaen' by Bwncath

Favourite animal: Dog (lemon beagle)

What do you do? Writer

WHY ARE YOU CONTRIBUTING TO THE ANTHOLOGY?

Representation is very important, especially for young people. It's a privilege to get to share my experiences in the hope that they will help/inspire others.

Sports

Sports day: the nightmare that comes along once a year. How can I avoid it this time? Mam comes to wake me up in the morning but here I am playing the most important role of my life: a sick child. I cough and sniff, put on a low voice that encourages sympathy. *Cwtch* back into my blanket so no one can tear it away from me. But Mam destroys my plans.

"I can't stay home to look after you today so you'll have to go to school." She offers me a handful of tablets and a special lunchbox containing chocolate and an extra half of tuna sandwich.

I arrive at school, disappointed with my failure. How can I get out of this? I hide my PE kit at the back of the registration class, explaining to Sir that I've left it at home.

"No matter," he says. "I'm sure there'll be something in the lost property box for you to wear." There's a solution for everything today.

Last chance to escape. I write a note "from Mam" in my school diary and sign it with the fake signature I've been practising since Year 7.

My child is ill so will not be able to participate today. Thank you.

Perfect.

Lesson 1. Boys play basketball. Girls play netball ... no thanks.

Lesson 2. Boys play rugby. Girls row ... no.

Lesson 3. Boys play five-a-side and girls play hockey. To be honest I enjoy hockey, but I'd prefer not to.

Lesson 4. Boys battle each other in a game of tug-of-war. Girls play it safe in the gym doing athletics ... you're joking!

Lesson 5. Everyone congregates in the hall to play ping-pong. First time I've seen the opposite sex since registration.

At last, a chance for me to play a game without worrying about who to play with or against. With mixed teams, it feels like there's finally a place for me. I don't have any skills in this field but at least I get a chance to do something. Fitness isn't so easy when you hate the body you live in. But for this hour, with the boys around me and ping-pong balls flying all over the place, I can imagine I'm one of them. One hour out of the twenty-four where I don't feel wrong. Well, less wrong than usual.

Shirts

Last day of school and everyone can't wait for the final bell to ring. This is the moment half the year has been waiting for. The first moment they get to leave education. No more homework or boring essays. Say goodbye to the harsh teachers who obviously hate children, and farewell to the good teachers who really did make a difference.

Everyone's signing their friends' navy polo shirts with gold, silver and copper Sharpies. The exact same pack of three everyone bought from their local shops. But, of course, the art students sign with fancy, expensive white Posca pens. "Complements the navy," according to them … It's clear we'll miss some more than others. Names start to fill up class by class and until a pen is placed in my hand and a back faces me like a canvas.

What should I write?

I have a new name no one knows yet. I've been signing my work with my surname, Drayton, since the beginning of the year. Exams use a GCSE number anyway so your name doesn't matter to them. Workbooks and homework don't even get the pleasure of having a full name on them.

I can't write my given name, the old name that gives me a headache. The name associated with the things that are best forgotten. The version of myself I would like to bury in a forest far, far away so that no one can ever find "her" again. It's not her I want them to remember. In the future, when my classmates find their shirts in a box or in the back of a drawer collecting dust, I don't want them to remember the sad, complicated person who was never confident or comfortable in their own body.

I need everyone to know that I'm proud and strong as the person I am going to grow to be. The new boy they don't know yet. But they will!

LEO x

My name is **Iseult**

ABOUT ME

Pronouns: She/They

From: Newport

Interests: Making, producing and releasing music. Playing Minecraft.

Sexuality: Lesbian.

Three words to describe yourself: Creative, charismatic and funny

MY FAVOURITE THINGS

Favourite song: 'Give Yourself a Try' - The 1975

Favourite animal: Lamb

What do you do? Studying Media and Welsh

WHY ARE YOU CONTRIBUTING TO THE ANTHOLOGY?

I hope that sharing my experiences can contribute to a collective narrative, fostering a sense of safety and understanding for future generations of young queer individuals.

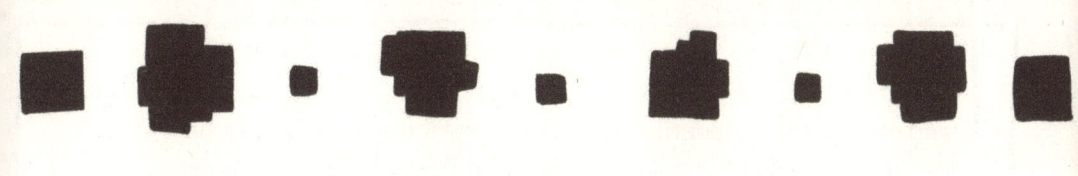

When I was thirteen, I began to realise my attraction to girls. Understanding and embracing my identity proved to be the most challenging journey. Accepting oneself is a daily struggle and finding comfort within myself has been a gradual process. However, I've learnt that staying true to who I am is paramount. Navigating societal expectations, especially regarding labels, has been particularly difficult. It's as if society demands clarity for their own comprehension, but internal exploration can be murky and complex.

I grew up in a Christian household, regularly attending a small Baptist church since childhood. Given my spiritual beliefs, I often grappled with feelings of worthlessness, influenced by societal portrayals suggesting disapproval of the queer community within religious circles. While undoubtedly there are individuals who hold such views, my personal experience shows that this isn't the only narrative. My family and community have shown nothing but unconditional love and acceptance towards me, regardless of my identity. At thirteen I confided in most of my friends about my sexuality but concealed it from many family members and classmates. The fear of potential reactions weighed heavily on me. However, I discovered that reality often differs from our worst fears. While I anticipated negative responses from those close to me, their reactions were far more accepting and supportive than I had imagined.

Regrettably, some memories from my school years are tinged with sadness. Around the age of fifteen or sixteen, certain boys in my year discovered my sexuality. Their reactions were hurtful, as they resorted to name-calling and made my daily life challenging. Reflecting on those moments now, I feel a hint of amusement at their immaturity. However, there's a lingering pang of hurt from one incident: a classmate threw chewing gum in my hair while calling me a dyke. Although I tried to brush it off and reassure the school authorities that everything was fine, in hindsight I wish I had spoken up. Addressing such behaviour could have prevented similar incidents in the future, and perhaps the school would have been better equipped to handle such situations. Openly LGBTQ+ individuals were scarce in my school, and I could count them on one hand. Therefore, I urge anyone facing similar challenges to speak out, not only for themselves but also for future generations. Every instance of discrimination or harassment deserves to be taken seriously and addressed promptly.

Following my GCSEs, I made the decision to leave school and enrol in a nearby college to pursue my A levels. The choice to forgo sixth form stemmed from my passion for continuing my journey as a second-language Welsh learner, a subject my previous school did not offer at A level. Though leaving the familiar environment of school initially sparked anxiety, I harbour no regrets about my decision. College provided a refreshing change, offering a diverse community where I found many peers with whom I could relate. Despite a slight apprehension, I eventually opened up to my new friends about my sexuality. To my relief, honesty deepened our connections, allowing me to be my authentic self without fear of judgement. One friend confided in me about her own struggles with identity, expressing curiosity about her sexuality and a desire to explore beyond past relationships with boys. I felt privileged that she felt comfortable sharing such intimate thoughts with me. Our friendship, while initially not as close as one might expect given such revelations, blossomed as she recognised my openness and acceptance. Unlike past experiences in school, where gossip spread like wildfire, she knew I wouldn't betray her trust or sensationalise her personal journey.

Upon entering university, I found myself surrounded by a similarly accepting and loving circle of friends, with many engaging in open discussions about their own journeys of self-discovery, including questions about their sexuality. This environment fostered a deeper understanding within me that the process of self-discovery is ongoing and universal.

It wasn't until my university years that I began to contemplate my gender identity and how I wished to express myself. Acknowledging my preferred pronouns, she/they, was a step I initially struggled with, resisting it internally for some time. However, connecting with others who shared similar experiences helped me embrace and understand myself more fully.

While I haven't yet discussed this topic with my family, it remains a deeply personal and sensitive matter for me. I am hopeful that, when the time is right, they will approach it with understanding and compassion. Reflecting on my own journey, if I could offer advice to my younger self, it would be to stress the importance of taking the coming-out process at my own pace. It's crucial not to feel pressured by external influences, especially if those pressures stem from a partner or societal expectations. The most significant thing is to stay authentic to oneself, valuing personal happiness and well-being as top priorities above all else. It's essential to remember that everyone's journey is unique, and there's no one-size-fits-all approach to coming out.

My name is Loti

ABOUT ME

Pronouns: She/Her

From: Abergavenny

Interests: Running, climbing, reading

Sexuality: Bisexual.

Three words to describe yourself: Strong, happy, determined

MY FAVOURITE THINGS

Favourite song: 'Viva La Vida' by Coldplay

Favourite animal: Giraffe

What do you do? Studying Politics and International Relations at Aberystwyth University

WHY ARE YOU CONTRIBUTING TO THE ANTHOLOGY?

I believe that if one person reading this realises that what they feel isn't wrong or weird, then I'd feel like I'd succeeded in the goal I set for my piece.

Maybe

Sometimes trying to understand who I am is like trying to separate strings tied up in a big ball of wool. You try and unpick all the pieces to create a pretty picture that can be fitted neatly into somebody else's idea of who you should be. I've spent most of my life trying to fit myself into that neat box; I had a vision of what being Welsh was and my bisexuality never seemed to fit into the picture. I think sometimes it's easier to try and ignore it, maybe in a way that's different to being gay or lesbian. You can try and convince yourself that that's not what you are: after all, you like guys too so why should you listen to those other thoughts? Maybe you try harder to push the thoughts in your head away, maybe you try and push away those "maybes". After all, maybe you're a person who's never seen someone like you before. And then when you do, your representation comes in dribs and drabs through American sitcoms or British TV shows. Maybe you can't imagine that a person like you can fit into this community. Maybe life as a Welsh bisexual can seem isolating and scary.

Maybe when your friend jokes that you're gayer than her because of the number of checked shirts you own your breath starts to go and the world feels like it's closing in. Maybe you don't understand why you feel that way because you've told yourself again and again that you're definitely straight. Absolutely. One hundred per cent. You try and figure what you've been doing wrong, what vibe you're giving off. Maybe you change yourself, so nobody makes that assumption again.

Maybe you grow up and realise that this is definitely not a phase; this is here to stay. You remind yourself each morning that you're not insane, that you're not wrong, that what you are is an OK thing to be. You put flag stickers on your laptop to remind yourself every day that you're good as you are. Maybe you beat yourself up because you can't change. Maybe you have a distant dream that you can wake up and are straight or gay because both options feel so simple compared to where you are. Maybe you go to the Eisteddfod and see the merchandise with "Mam a Dad" and know you don't quite fit in. You visit the recently added queer stand and find gays and lesbians and you're happy. But maybe it's an empty kind of happiness because you know that even though this stand wouldn't have existed five years ago there's still no one there like you. Maybe you feel a little bit like a sheep that someone placed in the rainforest by accident; everyone else seems to know who they are and you wander around aimlessly, trying to work it out.

Maybe you have your guard up in every conversation you have. Maybe regular conversations about fancying people, nights out and dates feel like walking on a tightrope. Maybe you breathe a little easier when someone says they're from Cardiff or London because you know the chances are that they'll have met someone like you before. That what you are to them isn't strange or weird or unnatural. Maybe you've spent most of your life coming out again and again and again because people assume that you're gay or straight based on who you're dating. Because for them there is no in-between, maybe there's no pretty box for them to put you in when you're Welsh and bisexual. Somehow, you're defined even more by the person you date than who you are yourself. Maybe you get a sinking feeling that in the back of some people's minds who you are will always be thought of as a phase. That they'll feel better when they can put you back into a neat little box.

Sometimes maybe you think about how lucky you are. You have friends that knew who they were before you. Who hugged you and let you cry and rant and find yourself. You know that you have parents who love every piece of who you are. Whose biggest worry is if the world will hurt you, who warn you to tread carefully about who to tell, who remind you that the world will not always be kind. That people will judge you for who you like and not the tons of other things about you. Maybe you feel lucky because you know that there are hundreds who don't have that. That there are people who are scared, who don't have a support system, who didn't get the acceptance you got.

Maybe you know that life won't always be easy. That declaring who you are to the world will never not be scary. But maybe you think about when you were a scared kid, and you didn't know what was going on. How you felt wrong and awkward and in a constant state of limbo. About how someone else might feel that way, too. Because maybe there's another scared girl out there who thinks she's wrong because she doesn't fit into a neat little box and maybe you can make the world less intimidating for her.

A TIMELINE OF

1845

1994

1982

1917

LGBTQIA+ people have always existed in Wales, even though they might not have necessarily used the labels that we do today. There are queer themes in the fourth branch of the *Mabinogi*, for example, as Math son of Mathonwy changes Gwydion and Gilfaethwy into animals of a different sex for three years.

1876

2004

1893

1696

1953

1931

1901

2001

WELSH QUEER HISTORY

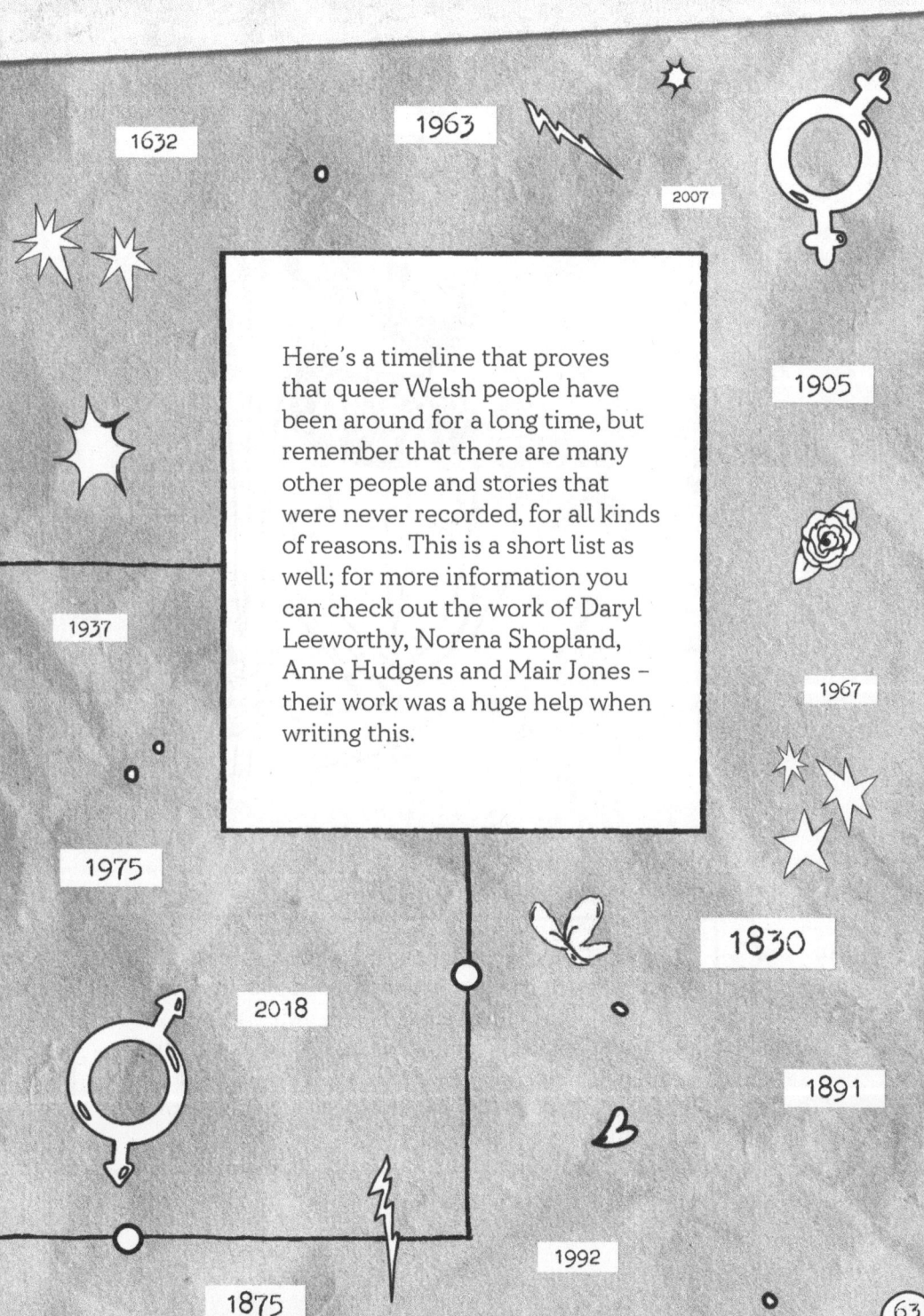

Here's a timeline that proves that queer Welsh people have been around for a long time, but remember that there are many other people and stories that were never recorded, for all kinds of reasons. This is a short list as well; for more information you can check out the work of Daryl Leeworthy, Norena Shopland, Anne Hudgens and Mair Jones - their work was a huge help when writing this.

1632
1963
2007
1905
1937
1967
1975
1830
2018
1891
1875
1992

The Middle Ages

In the Middle Ages the Welsh laws – the Laws of Hywel Dda – banned those "guilty" of sodomy from being witnesses in a court. The law also mentioned people classed as intersex.

1284

Edward II is born at Caernarfon Castle. More than one source suggests that Edward had been in love with one of his knights, Piers Gaveston. Later on, he had a close relationship with Hugh Despenser, the Lord of Glamorgan, as well. But there wasn't a happy ending to that relationship. Edward II lost his crown and Hugh was executed.

| 1320–1502 | Famous poets like Dafydd ap Gwilym and Gwerful Mechain discussed sex and gender as well, with poems like "*Cywydd y Gâl*" ("A Poem for the Penis") and "*Cywydd y Cedor*" ("An Ode to the Vagina"), discussing genitalia quite thoroughly...

| 1632 | Katharine Phillips, a famous and influential female poet, is born in London. She moved to Wales as a child and lived in Aberteifi as an adult. Her work discusses female relationships, closeness and eroticism.

1696 — Marged ferch Ifan, a harpist, smithy and shoemaker, is born near Beddgelert. Marged was known for her feats of strength and the fact that she didn't conform to traditional gender norms; she was a famous wrestler for one thing!

1778 — The "Ladies of Llangollen", Eleanor Charlotte Butler and Sarah Ponsonby, arrive at Llangollen and settle there after fleeing from Ireland. Both became famous, and had many celebrity visitors – including Anne Lister, the "first modern lesbian". They had a very close, loving relationship, though they didn't use the label "lesbian".

1790 — John Gibson is born in Conwy; he became known for his sculptures and was in a relationship with another artist, Penry Williams.

1802 — Penry Williams is born in Merthyr Tudful; he moved to Rome and had a distinguished career as an artist. He was known as a "close friend" to John Gibson.

1819 — Mary Charlotte Lloyd, a sculptor who studied with John Gibson, is born in Denbighshire. She was in a long-term relationship with the feminist Frances Power Cobbe and both were buried together at Llanelltyd.

1830 — Abel Jones, "*Y Bardd Crwst*" ("The Crust Poet") is born in Llanrwst. He who wrote a ballad about two cross-dressing women having sex with women called "The ballad of two young women from this parish that dressed themselves in the clothes of men, and went to a manor house to love two young ladies, who weren't known to them". It's rather graphic, considering the tastes of the time!

1839

Sarah Jane Rees or "Cranogwen" is born in Llangrannog. She became a famous Welsh-language poet and editor. Her poem *"Fy Ffrynd"* ("My Friend") refers to her neighbour, Jane Thomas; the two were in a lifelong relationship and spent the last twenty years of Sarah's life living together.

1839-43

The Rebecca Riots take place, where men wore women's clothes and attacked tollhouses in protest against high tolls. There are other recorded examples across Britain of people dressing in gender-nonconforming ways to undermine social norms.

Amy Dillwyn, author and entrepreneur, is born in Swansea; She was famous for wearing unconventional clothes for women of her time and smoking cigars. She referred to Olive Talbot as her wife and would often send her love letters.

1845

Rachel Barrett, a suffragist and editor, is born in Caerfyrddin. She became romantically involved with another woman, I. A. R. Wylie, who contributed to the newspaper that Barrett edited. In 1928, Barrett gave her full support to Radclyffe Hall, the author of a book called *The Well of Loneliness* that discussed a gay relationship. Radclyffe Hall had been accused of publishing obscene material.

1874

Henry Cyril Paget, the 5th Marquess of Anglesey, is born. There's a lot of discussion about the sexuality of Henry the colourful marquess, his obsession with performance and art, and his amazing costumes and jewels. Though there's no direct evidence of his sexuality (his family burned his letters after his death) it's clear that his gender identity was fluid, especially considering the norms of the period.

1875

1876 — Gwen John, a talented artist who was raised in Tenby, is born. She had sexual relationships with men and women, and her work portrays the bodies of both sexes.

1883 — Margaret Haig Mackworth, 2nd Viscountess of Rhondda, is born in London – her relationships with women and men are recorded.

1890

Nina Hamnett, an artist and author from Tenby, is born. She would later be called the "Queen of Bohemia", partly because she openly discussed her bisexual relationships.

1891

Kate Roberts, known as the "Queen of Welsh Literature", is born in Rhosgadfan – she wrote many classic Welsh novels such as *Traed Mewn Cyffion* (Feet in Chains). There are hints in her writing that she might have been bisexual and many of her books offer queer readings. She also noted in a letter after kissing another woman that "Nothing else has given me more pleasure than this."

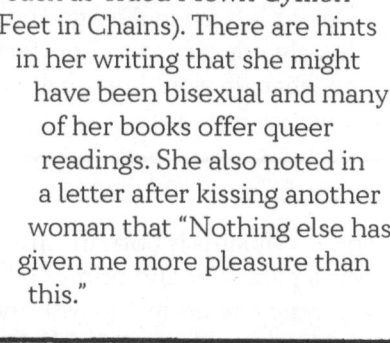

1893 — Ivor Novello, actor, composer and playwright, is born in Cardiff. He was an openly gay man and spent thirty-five years in a relationship with his partner Bobbie Andrews.

1899 — Tom Davies is born in Abergwynfi; he became known as a "female impersonator", performing in a similar style to what we would now call drag. He had a long career across Britain.

1900 — Morris T. Williams is born in Groeslon, North Wales. He was a publisher and printer by trade. He had a close physical relationship with the poet Edward Prosser Rhys and he married Kate Roberts in 1928.

1901 — Edward Prosser Rhys is born in the Mynydd Bach area; a poet, editor and journalist. He's most famous for his poem *"Atgof"* ("Memory"), which chronicles queer experiences.

1904

John Gwilym Jones is born in Groeslon; he's known for his work as a playwright, author and lecturer. A number of his works feature queer themes, most famously the drama *Ac Eto Nid Myfi* (And Yet Not Myself), and academics like Mihangel Morgan have argued that he wasn't heterosexual.

Angus McBean is born in Monmouthshire. He was a famous portrait photographer – however, his career was temporarily ruined when he was jailed in 1942 for "criminal acts of homosexuality". He later became internationally famous and photographed The Beatles amongst others.

1905

Emlyn Williams, a bisexual author and playwright, is born in Flintshire.

1909

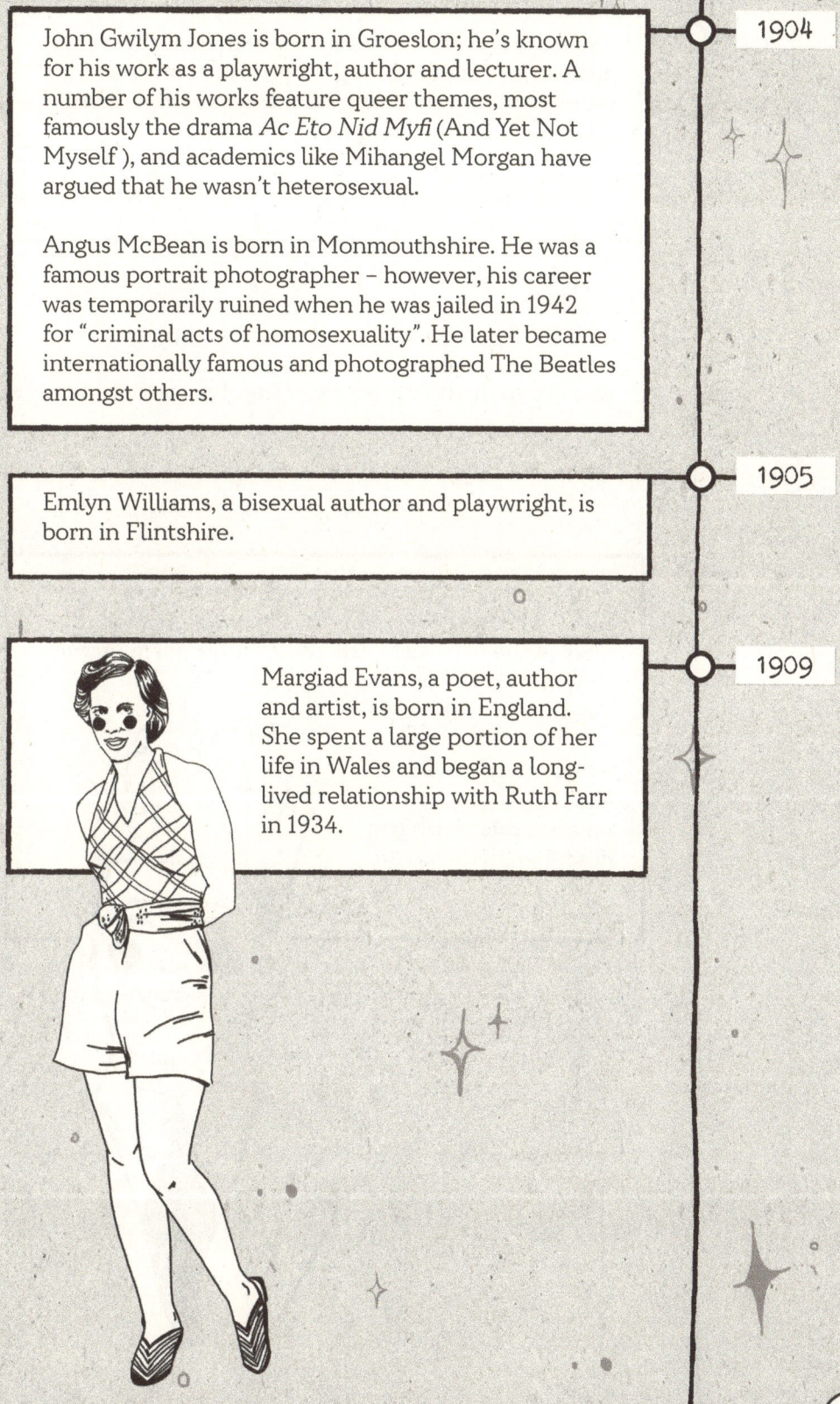

Margiad Evans, a poet, author and artist, is born in England. She spent a large portion of her life in Wales and began a long-lived relationship with Ruth Farr in 1934.

1917 — Leo Abse is born; he was an MP from Cardiff who campaigned on behalf of gay rights. He played a large part in the journey towards achieving the rights that the LGBTQIA+ community have today.

1918 — John Randell is born in Penarth. An academic and psychologist, he discussed many aspects of the LGBTQIA+ community and was the first person to write a dissertation about trans people in Wales. He also set up the first gender identity clinic in Britain.

1924 — At the astoundingly young age of twenty-three, Edward Prosser Rhys wins the Crown, a prestigious prize at the National Eisteddfod, for his poem *"Atgof"* ("Memory"). He's thought to have been a bisexual man who had a relationship with Morris T. Williams, and it's believed that their physical relationship is described in the poem.

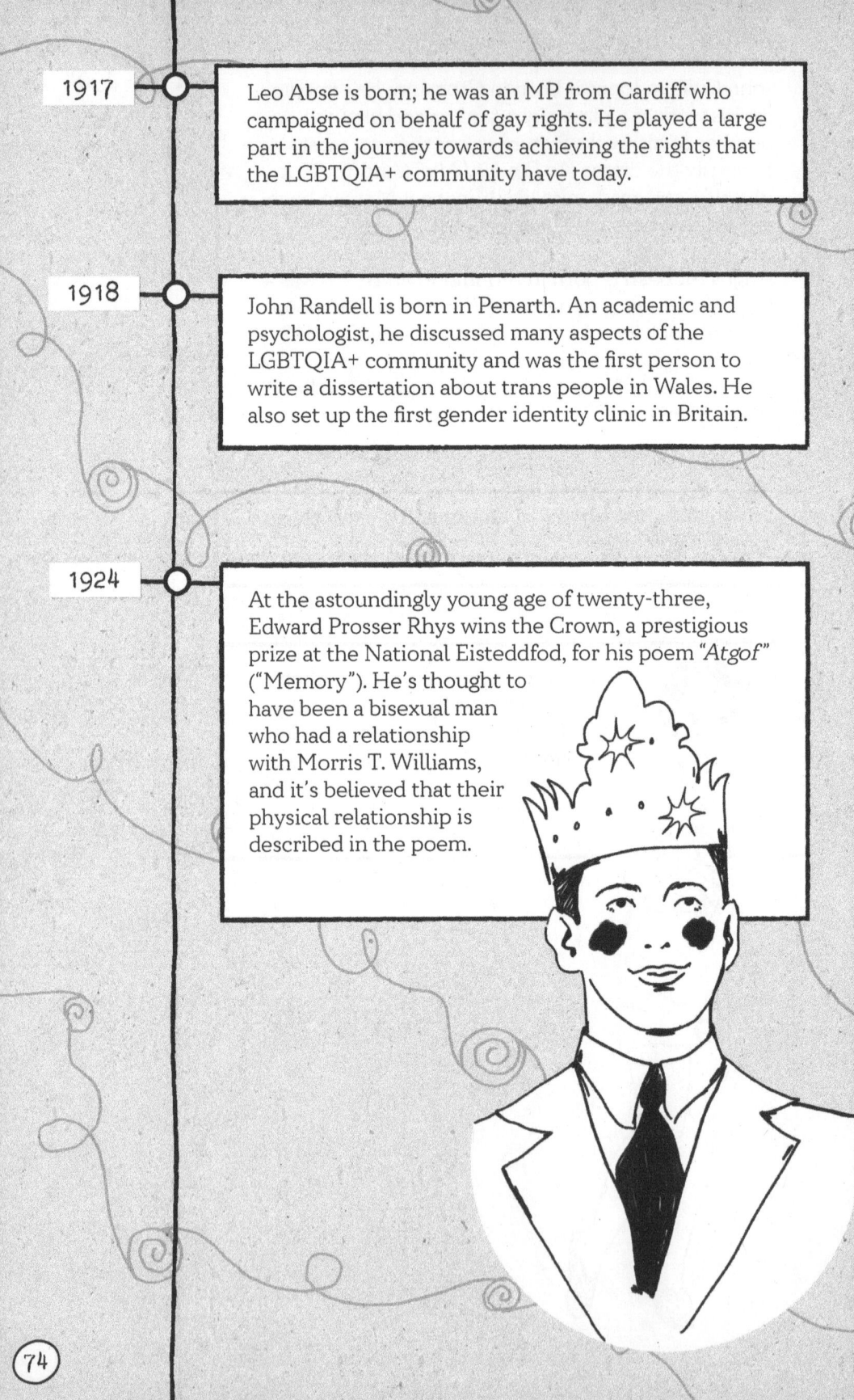

1931

Jo Opie, campaigner, anarchist and feminist, is born. She was a member of many organisations – such as the Lesbian and Gay Freedom Movement.

Illtyd Harrington is born in Merthyr Tudful; he was politically active for his whole life and enjoyed an openly gay life with his partner Chris Downes for thirty years, even when being gay was still criminalised.

1937

Gloria Jenkins is born; she founded the Welsh branch of Fflag (Families and Friends of Lesbians and Gays) and was one of the first co-chairs of Stonewall Cymru.

1938

John Davies is born in the Rhondda. He was a well-respected historian and came out publicly on S4C as bisexual.

1939 — Wena Parry is born; she is a trans woman who went to the European Court of Human Rights to challenge the Gender Recognition Act when she couldn't get a gender recognition certificate without divorcing her wife, Anita.

1940 — Griffith Vaughan Williams is born in Bangor; he was an activist, journalist and campaigner. He spent much of his life campaigning for the rights of LGBTQIA+ people. He was an early member of the Campaign for Homosexual Equality (CHE) that was formed in 1969.

1953 — Desmond Donnelly, MP for Pembroke, calls for an inquiry into why being gay is still illegal in the UK. Within a year, the Wolfenden Report would begin. This report would be a small step towards equality for the LGBTQIA+ community. Another Welshman, Goronwy Rees, was an important member of the report's panel, arguing that gay men should be allowed to give evidence.

| | 1955 |

Mihangel Morgan, a gay author and academic, is born; his work is known for exploring LGBTQIA+ themes.

| | 1956 |

John Sam Jones, author and campaigner, is born in Meirionnydd. His work discusses a wide range of gay experience, including the effect that a homophobic community can have on gay individuals.

| | 1963 |

Russell T. Davies is born in Swansea; he will later go on to write numerous television dramas with LGBTQIA+ themes.

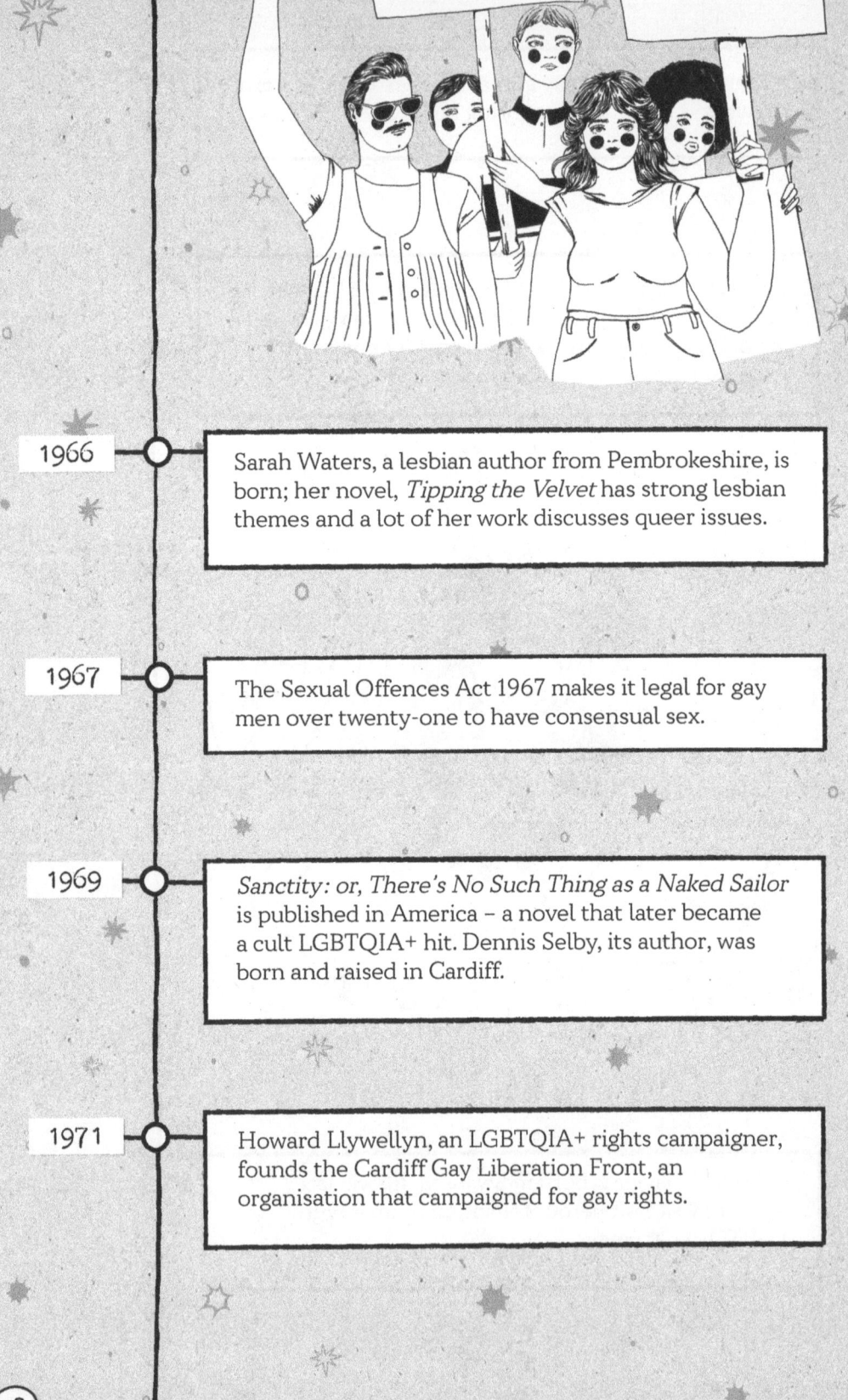

1966 — Sarah Waters, a lesbian author from Pembrokeshire, is born; her novel, *Tipping the Velvet* has strong lesbian themes and a lot of her work discusses queer issues.

1967 — The Sexual Offences Act 1967 makes it legal for gay men over twenty-one to have consensual sex.

1969 — *Sanctity: or, There's No Such Thing as a Naked Sailor* is published in America – a novel that later became a cult LGBTQIA+ hit. Dennis Selby, its author, was born and raised in Cardiff.

1971 — Howard Llywellyn, an LGBTQIA+ rights campaigner, founds the Cardiff Gay Liberation Front, an organisation that campaigned for gay rights.

1972

Jan Morris, author and essayist, travels to Morocco for gender reassignment surgery. She wrote about her experiences in *Conundrum*. She was forced to divorce her wife but they continued to live together, becoming civil partners in 2008.

1975

The term "*hoyw*" is coined in Welsh. Ann Beynon, a student at the time asked Gwyn Thomas, a lecturer in the Welsh Department at Bangor University, what the Welsh word was for "gay". "*Hoyw*" was the answer. That year at the National Eisteddfod, badges stating "*Hawliau Hoywon*" ("Rights for Gay People") were handed out.

1977 — Plaid Cymru, the Welsh nationalist party, discuss LGBTQIA+ rights in their yearly conference; in 1978 the party will state their opposition to discrimination on the basis of race, belief, sexuality or language.

1982 — Terrence, or Terry, Higgins dies of AIDS, one of the first people in the UK to do so. He was originally from Pembrokeshire. The Terrence Higgins Trust charity was established in his memory.

1984-85 — Lesbians and Gays Support the Miners is set up to support the National Union of Miners and works closely with communities in South Wales during strike action. Eleven groups were formed nationally, with the London-based one alone raising £22,500 (a lot of money in the eighties!) to support the strikers.

1988

The Local Government Act 1988 is passed, also known as "Section 28". This discriminatory act makes discussing LGBTQIA+ people effectively illegal in schools.

1992

The Welsh gay rights group, *Cylch* (Circle) campaigns at the National Eisteddfod.

Phone-based support groups, Gwynedd and Bangor Lesbian Line and the Gay Gwynedd Line, combine to create a counselling service.

The Triangle Housing Association is set up in Cardiff to help local LGBTQIA+ people get housing.

RHAID NEWID POPETH
Medd
HOYWON A LESBIAID

1993

The Welsh-language film *Gadael Lenin* (*Leaving Lenin*) is broadcast; amongst the characters is a young gay man coming to terms with his sexuality.

1994 — The age of consent for sex between men is lowered from twenty-one to eighteen.

1995 — *Dafydd*, a television drama about a gay man, is broadcast on S4C.

1997 — The first lesbian kiss is broadcast on the Welsh-language soap opera, *Pobol y Cwm*.

1999

Queer as Folk by Russell T. Davies is broadcast.

Cardiff Mardi Gras, now known as Pride Cymru, is formed.

2000

Wales has its first openly lesbian mayor – Jaci Taylor in Aberystwyth.

Stonewall and the Welsh Government discuss forming the Lesbian and Gay Forum for Wales, with John Sam Jones and Gloria Jenkins chairing.

2001

The age of consent for sex between men is lowered to sixteen, in line with heterosexual couples.

2002

The law changes to allow gay, lesbian, trans and unmarried heterosexual people to adopt children.

The first Welsh Lesbian and Gay Forum conference is held, with over 200 people attending.

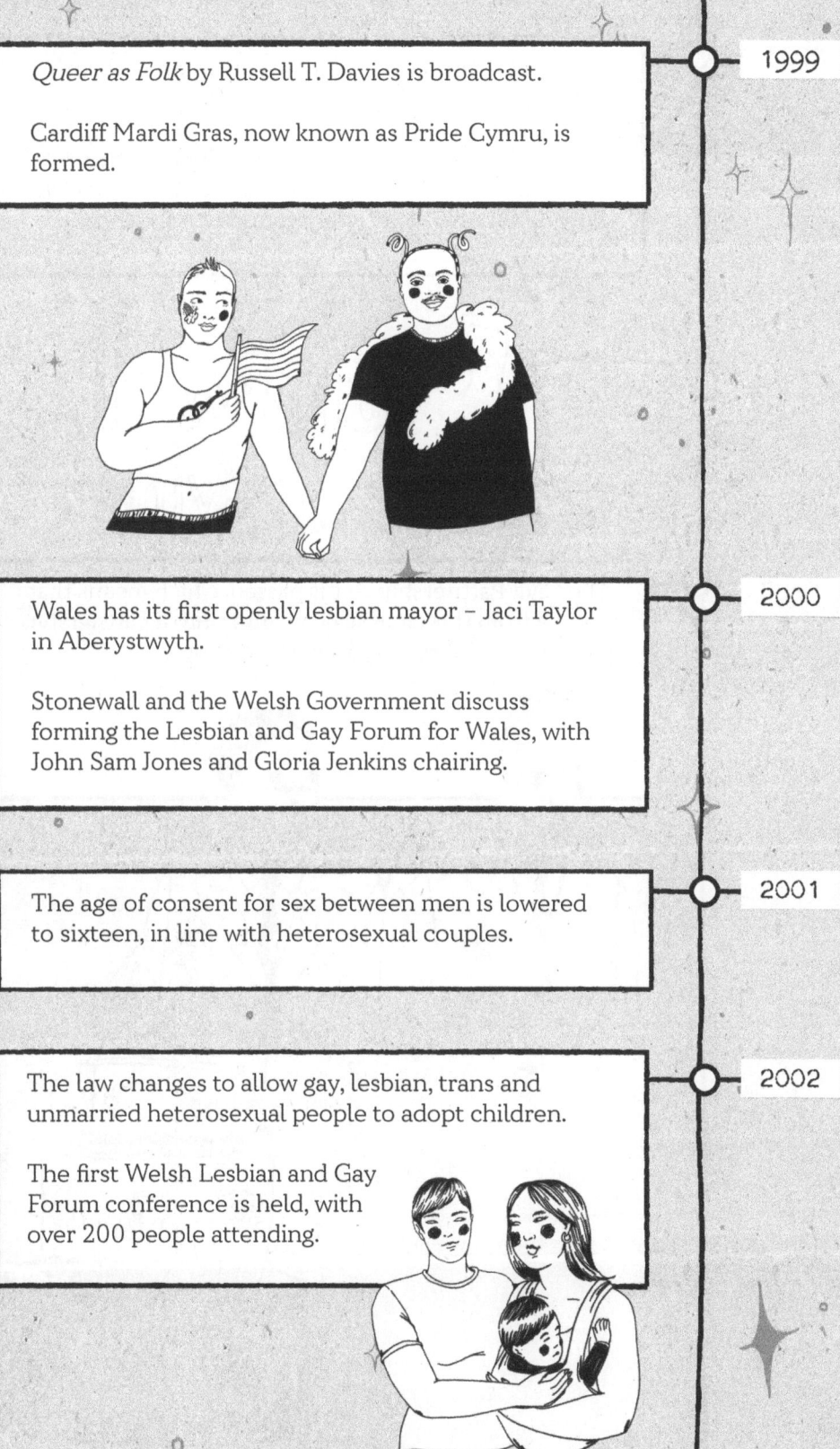

2003

Stonewall Cymru is formed by uniting the Lesbian and Gay Forum and Stonewall in Wales.

Section 28 is taken from legislation, though thanks to the work of the Lesbian and Gay Forum the Welsh Government had effectively got rid of it in 2002.

Stonewall Cymru

2004

The Civil Partnership Act is passed, which means that people from the same sex can enter into a partnership that has similar rights to a married couple.

The Iris Prize is set up in Cardiff; it's an international film prize that celebrates LGBTQIA+ films.

2007

Pride North Wales is founded.

2011

2018 — The first year of Mas ar y Maes (Out on the Field) at the National Eisteddfod. This is the first time LGBTQIA+ events get special attention there.

MAS AR Y MAES

2023 — *Cwiar na Nog*, a special place for young queer people, is established at the Urdd Eisteddfod.

And that's a very short history of queer Wales; we haven't included everyone or everything and, of course, our history is still growing!

WHAT IS PRIDE?

It was direct action that started Pride. In the early hours of the 28th of June, 1969, the Stonewall Riots started after the police raided the Stonewall Inn, a gay bar in New York.

For five days, the riots spread as the anger the LGBTQIA+ community felt came to the surface. We were discriminated against and victimised as a community.

Following the riots, many organisations were formed and, a year later, some of them came together to remember what had happened and to protest for more rights. The event was called the Christopher Street Day Parade at this time.

In 1972 Pride arrived in Britain with a rally in London that saw around 200 people on the streets, though, similar events had been held already.

In 1989 Stonewall was set up and, of course, the name reminds us of an important step in the battle for equality.

Much of the hard work happened in grass-roots communities and it was radical protest and direct action over decades that got us to where we are today. Pride is now a celebration of our community and a chance to socialise and enjoy ourselves – which is great, but we have to remember where we came from and that Pride was first and foremost a protest movement.

HOW THIS BOOK CAME ABOUT

A note for readers, parents, guardians, and teachers ...

We were given the opportunity to apply for funding from an inclusion and diversity grant offered by the Welsh Government. The money would enable us to research and develop content for a new book aimed at young people aged twelve and above. When our application was approved, the questions that immediately came to mind were:

- Where do we start?
- Where are the gaps in the market?
- What sort of book would this audience be interested in reading?

We decided to start by looking at some of the most recent statistics available from Wales and it very quickly became apparent that there had been a worrying increase in recorded hate crime.

Definition: hate crime is a crime, typically involving violence, that is motivated by prejudice.

The law recognises five types of hate crime on the basis of:

- Race
- Religion
- Disability
- Sexual orientation
- Transgender identity

Sometimes the same person can be a victim of **more than one** type of hate crime.

Data

The statistics below were published by the Home Office on 6 October 2022 and show that every Welsh police force had seen an increase in the number of hate crimes recorded.

Hate crime in Wales
Recorded crime by police force area

Police Force Area	2020/21 Total number of offences	2021/22 Total number of offences	% change	Hate crime rate per 1,000 population
North Wales	1,144	1,520	33%	2.2
Gwent	677	1,234	82%	2.1
South Wales	2,148	2,717	26%	2
Dyfed-Powys	685	824	20%	1.6
Wales	4,654	6,295	35%	2

Source: Home Office, 6 October

BBC

This bar graph shows a worrying increase over a six-year period.

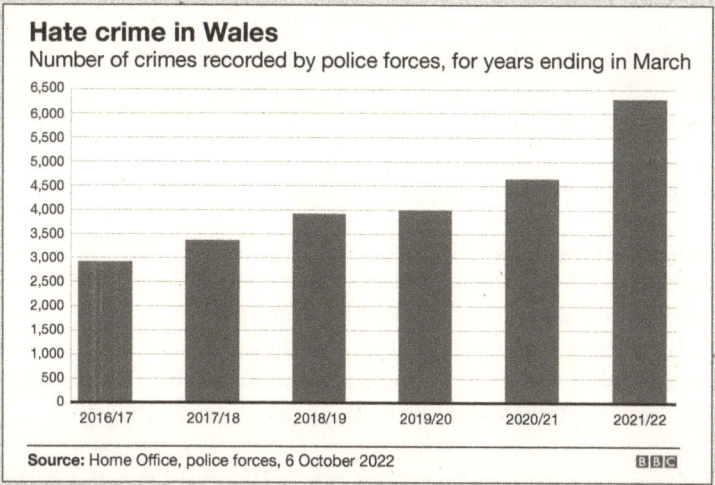

There could be all sorts of reasons for these increases, such as the police forces taking these types of crimes more seriously and more cases being recorded. But we felt that this overall trend was concerning and we decided to dig deeper into the data.

This table breaks down the hate crime data for England and Wales into five categories.

Hate crime strand	2018/19	2019/20	2020/21	2021/22
Race	77,850	[x]	90,909	108,476
Religion	8,460	[x]	6,288	8,602
Sexual orientation	14,161	[x]	18,239	25,639
Disability	8,052	[x]	9,690	13,905
Transgender	2,253	[x]	2,728	4,262
Total number of offences	104,765	112,633	122,256	153,536

Source: Police recorded crime, Home Office

No data was documented during 2019/20 due to the Covid pandemic. However, over a period of four years, reported religious hate crime rose by 1.7% and race hate crimes rose by 39%. There was an increase of 73% in reported disability crimes and an increase of 81% in reported crimes based on sexual orientation. Reported hate crimes against transgender people rose by 89% across England and Wales.

As is common with many types of crime, these statistics only provide a glimpse of the reality. Other government statistics suggest fewer than one in ten LGBTQIA+ people report hate crimes or incidents.

This data shows a sad fact: that hate crime and, more specifically, crime involving sexual orientation and gender identity, has significantly increased in Wales. It's an increase that:

- means harm and distress is caused to people whose freedom to be themselves and to express themselves needs to be protected and whose safety and security must be ensured.
- involves perpetrators who limit and damage their own prospects by expressing views and conducting themselves in ways that are misguided and who need to be supported to change.

Moved by this, we discussed whether our book could help to address the situation, by promoting and encouraging understanding, inclusion and consideration in people while they are young.

We thought we should try!

Our aim:

Our team decided that one of the best ways to draw people in is through storytelling. Everyone loves a story. And if it's true ... all the better! We wanted to include as many stories as possible, and so we invited numerous people to create the content, which would provide a balanced and representative account of the realities some people face.

Our aim was to include personal experiences from the LGBTQIA+ community, told in peer-to-peer style by our authors to young readers in an easy-to-read and beautifully presented book.

Our vision:

We realised this could be a brilliant opportunity to reach out and involve young people who had never written publicly before. We believed that we could provide a positive and empowering creative environment that would enable contributors to learn new skills and write their personal stories in their own authentic voices. We were clear that we didn't want this to become a textbook. Instead, our aspiration was to share knowledge about the LGBTQIA+ community through storytelling and real-life events. By reading about the honest experiences of this minority group, we hope to enable the majority to become more understanding.

The statistics speak for themselves. Hate crime has increased.
We believe that there is a desperate need for more education, resulting in a better-informed population. Our sincere hope is that this book will contribute in some small way to achieving this goal.

To close:

This has been a tremendous task and possibly the biggest project on which we have ever worked. But the journey has been worthwhile and the reward (both individually and collectively) has been even greater.

We believe the final outcome is an anthology of fresh, honest, heartfelt stories that we hope will resonate with readers. Even if you are not part of the LGBTQIA+ community, we hope that these personal narratives are relatable and fascinating to read.

Our thanks to Llŷr and Megan, who trained, mentored and empowered each contributor to write their own story to a level where they were approved to be published; to Mari Phillips for her wonderful illustrations; Richard Pritchard for his brilliant scrapbook-style design; Books Council of Wales and the Welsh Government for providing the funding and support for this project; and, of course, to all the amazing contributors who helped write this book.

And finally ... thank *you* for reading!

Team RILY

SUPPORT

Being young and queer isn't always easy, and that's normal. If you need help, don't suffer in silence; there are organisations and people out there that can help you. You're never alone.

The information below is correct at the time of publication, but of course things can change. Searching online for "wales help lgbtq" can help you find resources if our information is out of date.

This is a short list:

Childline
Help for everyone under nineteen. Call 0800 1111 any time. There's more help on their website as well.

MindLineTrans +
0300 330 5468. Help with mental health; an anonymous space to chat for those who are trans, agender, genderfluid or non-binary.

MindOut
A mental health service for queer people. Call 01273 234839 or email info@mindout.org.uk. They also have a chat function on their website.

PAPYRUS
A national organisation that aims to stop suicide amongst young people. If you or anyone you know is considering taking their own life, PAPYRUS can support you.
      Call 0800 068 4141 or 0808 115 1505, or text 07860 039 967.

Samaritans
Anonymous help for whatever is worrying you. Call twenty-four hours a day on 116 123.

Switchboard
A support line. Call 0800 0119 100 from 10 a.m. to 10 p.m. or email hello@switchboard.lgbt. Their website also has a chat function.

Umbrella Cymru
You can text 07520 645700 for help or call them on 0300 302 3670. If no one answers, you can leave a message with your details and someone will get back to you.
      You can also email support@umbrellacymru.co.uk.

LGBTQIA+ ORGANISATIONS

Constellation
A well-being project for young people between the ages of twelve to twenty-six that are trans, non-binary or exploring their gender in Cardiff.
   Call 029 20344776 for more information.

G(end)er Swap
G(end)er Swap is an outreach organisation and community interest company that supports trans and gender non-conforming individuals to access clothes and community. Their website has resources, practical information, a shop and discusses their work.

GISDA
A homelessness charity based in North Wales that offers help to young people between the ages of sixteen and twenty-five – they have an LGBTQIA+ support service as well, including a club that meets regularly. Call 01286 671153.

Glitter Cymru
An organisation for queer global-majority individuals that offers meetings and events.

Impact LGBT+
A Cardiff-based youth service that offers a safe space to meet people from the same community as you. Email lgbt@cathays.org.uk for more information.

LGBT+ Cymru Helpline
Support, help and advice for LGBTQIA+ individuals and their friends and family. They offer therapy and counselling services and their helpline is open between 10 a.m. and 3 p.m. each Wednesday. If you phone beyond these hours and leave a message with your details, then someone will get back to you. The number is 0800 917 9996.
   They also run the GoodVibes scheme in Swansea, a safe space for socialising if you're between the ages of eleven and twenty-five. Email info@LGBTCymru.org.uk for more information, or you can call 01792 650777.

Trans Aid Cymru
Help for trans, non-binary and intersex people from their own community. Trans Aid also arranges events and offers grants to help with various costs. Email enquiries@transaid.cymru for more information.

Tŷ Pride
A twenty-four-hour service to help young LGBTQIA+ people that are under threat of homelessness. Find more information online.

Umbrella Cymru
Help, support, counselling and advocacy. Call 0300 302 3670 and if no one answers, you can leave a message with your details and someone will get back to you. You can also email support@umbrellacymru.co.uk.

Unique Transgender Network
A voluntary group that offers help and support for trans people in North Wales and Cheshire.

Viva LGBT+
Youth groups around Denbighshire, Conwy, Flintshire, Anglesey and Wrexham for young LGBTQIA+ people aged eleven to twenty-five or those who are questioning. Contact 01745 357941 or email info@vivalgbt.co.uk.

The websites of Stonewall Cymru and Pride Cymru also have useful pages about help and support.